LOOK UP!

Written by
Nathan Bryon

Illustrated by
Dapo Adeola

To my favourite stars in the universe -
Mum, Dad, Bro and my supernova Theresa - N.B.

Dedicated with love to my five nieces,
especially Sarah, the inspiration behind Rocket.
May you all be forever curious about
the wonders of the world - D.A.

PUFFIN BOOKS

UK | USA | Canada | Ireland | Australia | India | New Zealand | South Africa

Puffin Books is part of the Penguin Random House group of companies
whose addresses can be found at global.penguinrandomhouse.com.

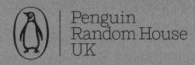

Penguin
Random House
UK

First published 2019

006

Text copyright © Nathan Bryon, 2019
Illustrations copyright © Dapo Adeola, 2019

The moral right of the author and illustrator has been asserted

Printed in Italy
A CIP catalogue record for this book is available from the British Library

ISBN: 978–0–241–34584–9

All correspondence to: Puffin Books, Penguin Random House Children's
80 Strand, London WC2R 0RL

Every night before bed,
I set up my telescope
and look up at the stars.

Mum tells me that I never stop looking up and my head is always floating *in* the clouds.

But she can't tell me that I **LOOK UP**
more than my big brother, Jamal,
LOOKS DOWN at his silly phone.

Jamal says I'm called Rocket because I've got fiery breath.

But Mum says it's because a famous rocket blasted off into space the day I was born!

All I know is that one day I'm going to be the greatest **astronaut, star-catcher, space-traveller** who has ever lived, like Mae Jemison, the first African-American woman in space.

DID YOU KNOW

Mae Jemison went into orbit around Earth in the space shuttle Endeavour, even though she is scared of heights!

I'm totally prepared.

I've defied gravity . . .

captured rare and exotic life forms . . .

and built a ship to the stars!

For today's mission, I'm going to see something incredible:

THE PHOENIX METEOR SHOWER!

I want **everyone** to see it with me,
so I've made some flyers to hand out!

Jamal is going to take me to the park to see the meteor shower. But first we have to go to the supermarket. While he's looking for the milk, I will be trying to find the astronaut food!

DID YOU KNOW meteor showers happen when Earth moves through the trail of dust left by a comet?

DID YOU KNOW most meteors are smaller than a grain of sand?

DID YOU KNOW meteors are bits of dust burning up in the atmosphere?

DID YOU KNOW the best time to see a meteor shower is when it's dark, with no clouds?

SUPER STORE

Buy! Buy! Buy!

In the supermarket, when
Cathy the cashier isn't looking,
I grab the microphone . . .

BE HEALTHY

Buy fresh fruit
in store now.

Tonight: come out and witness **THE AMAZING PHOENIX METEOR SHOWER!**

Everyone

LOOKS UP!

Cathy takes her
microphone back
as I hand out my flyers
to the other people
in the queue.

I think Jamal might be
a tiny bit cross with me.

THE PHOENIX
METEOR SHOWER
will come soon — we'd better
drop off the shopping and get
to the park fast!

"Oooops!"

"Ha ha!
That wouldn't have
happened if you had just
LOOKED UP!"

Now Jamal is even more cross
with me. And he says he won't
take me to the park any more!

But when we get home, Mum saves the day.
"Come on, Jamal," she says. "Put that phone down
and take your little sister to the park."

YES!

I jump up and do my famous victory dance around the house.

I grab my jet-pack rucksack,
but Jamal is still glued to his game.

"Wait till I've completed the level, Rocket!"
he grumbles.

As we're about to leave, the doorbell rings . . .

WOWSERS!

Everyone's here,
and they're all
holding my flyers.

"TO THE PARK!"

I yell at the
top of my lungs.
We're all
so excited!

My neck is aching from staring up into the night sky, but I won't stop.

I can't miss it!

Suddenly the park goes silent.
Even the birds are holding their breath.

Everyone points their telescopes
and binoculars up at the sky.

"I THINK
I SEE ONE!"

But it's just a plane flying overhead. Everyone moans and groans.

We wait

and wait

and **WAIT**.

It must be nearly time for the park to close. One by one people start to go home . . .

Maybe the Phoenix Meteor Shower
was just a myth.

Maybe that's why Jamal
didn't want to come along.

Maybe everyone is upset
with me for wasting their time.

I've never, ever
felt this sad before.

Jamal looks at me for
the first time today. It feels
like the first time ever.

"I've turned my phone off, sis,"
he says.

"I'm sorry for making
you wait in the freezing
cold for nothing, Jamal.

Let's go home."

Suddenly there's a big bright light in the sky!

THE PHOENIX METEOR SHOWER!

"I'm speechless," Jamal says. He pulls out his flask and gives me a warm cup of hot chocolate. Yummy!

We both sit down on the hill watching meteors
zoom across the sky.

I'm so happy we

LOOKED UP

and saw them together.

DID YOU KNOW one day I'm going to have a meteor shower named after me!